# THE MAN WITHOUT
# A COUNTRY

# THE MAN WITHOUT A COUNTRY

BY

EDWARD EVERETT HALE

NEW EDITION

WITH AN INTRODUCTION IN THE YEAR
OF THE WAR WITH SPAIN

BOSTON
LITTLE, BROWN, AND COMPANY
1925

# Introduction

THE war with Spain naturally carries back people's memories to the war of a generation ago. And young men may well compare their motives now with the motives of their fathers then.

It was curious at that time to see how some men who had consciences, and who had more than the average intelligence, could not at the first understand the sentiment of loyalty to one's country. There is a perfectly absurd statement by Charles Kingsley, in the preface to one of his books, in which he says that, while there can be loyalty to a king or a queen, there cannot be loyalty to one's country.

At the present moment, hundreds of thousands of fine young men are taking arms for the United States of America, for the country which they love as men love their fathers or their mothers.

In the Civil War, in a special crisis which I have described in the preface to this story, it seemed advisable to point in a parable the lesson of what love of country is. After six-and-thirty years, I may frankly say that I am proud that a desire has been expressed that that parable shall be reprinted.

This story of Philip Nolan was written in the darkest period of the Civil War. There were persons then who thought that if their advice had been taken there need have been no Civil War. There were persons whose every-day pursuits were greatly deranged by the Civil War. I suppose there are such persons now, who look on this war with Spain with a very unfriendly eye, because it disturbs all their plans, and because they think things could have been better done.

In this crisis, in 1863, an important

election was pending in Ohio. A man named Vallandigham, long since forgotten except from his connection with this matter, was the candidate of the party which opposed the National Government. This Mr. Vallandigham had said that he did not want to belong to a nation which would compel by arms the service of any of its citizens: he did not want to belong to the United States. General Burnside, who was the Union commander-in-chief in the West, with the powers of martial law, sent Mr. Vallandigham, with his compliments, to the rebel commander on the other side of the Ohio. He said that if Mr. Vallandigham did not want to live in the United States, the United States did not want to have him there, and presented him, with his best respects, to the commanding general of the enemy.

It was during the election which was to decide whether such a man should be the Governor of Ohio or not that I wrote the story of "The Man without a Country," hoping to quicken the patriotism of people who were called upon to support the general Government, not merely in arms, but by their sympathy, by their taxes, and by caring for the soldier. By an accident in publication, the story though in type was not printed till the Ohio election had passed for some months, and Mr. Vallandigham had been completely forgotten. But it proved that the lesson was a lesson gladly received. I have had letters from seamen who read it as they were lying in our blockade squadrons off the mouths of Southern harbors. I have had letters from men who read it just after the Vicksburg campaign. And in other ways I have had many illustrations of its having been of use in what I have a right to call the darkest period of the Republic.

To-day we are not in the darkest period of the Republic; but we are unexpectedly and unwillingly in war. This Nation never wishes to make war. Our whole policy is a policy of peace, and peace is the protection of the Christian civilization to which we are pledged. But, as ex-President Harrison said so well the other day, if you see a man abusing his wife or his child, if when you remonstrate with him he does not cease, if he goes on beating his wife or his child, you do not wait to send for a sheriff or a police officer, but you take him by force of arms and compel him to behave himself. In this case, this country is in a similar position with regard to the monarchy of Spain. This country has long protested against the cruelties of Spain's administration in Cuba and the inefficiency of that administration. There is cause enough for war in saying that we will not have a fever-bed of yellow fever directly to windward of us, against the poison of which we must struggle every year.

In any high view of international law, it is our duty to see that our neighbors are not starved to death. According to the customs of nations, the destruction of the Maine in a friendly harbor deserves some apology and reparation from the government of Spain, which that government has never chosen to give to us. For such reasons, the calm historical fact is that we are at war with Spain. In that war it is time again for young men and young women, and old men and old women, for all sorts of people, to understand that the Country is in itself an entity. It is a Being. The Lord God of nations has called it into existence, and has placed it here with certain duties in defence of the civilization of the world.

It was the intention of this parable, which describes the life of one man who tried to separate himself from his country, to show how terrible was his mistake.

It does not need now that a man should curse the United States, as Philip Nolan did, or that he should say he hopes he may never hear her name again, to make it desirable for him to consider the lessons which are involved in the parable of his life. The man who, by his sneers, or by looking backward, or by revealing his country's secrets to her enemy, delays for one hour peace between Spain and this Nation, is to all purposes "A Man without a Country." He has not damned the United States in a spoken oath.

All the same he is a dastard child.

At a moment like this, indeed, all of us ought to remember that there is a definite, visible Progress in the affairs of this world. Jesus Christ at the end of his life prayed to God that all men might become One, "As thou, Father, art in me, and I in thee, that they also may be one in us."

The history of the world for eighteen hundred and fifty-five years since he spoke has shown the steady fulfilment of the hope expressed in this prayer.

Men are nearer unity — they are nearer to being one — than they were then.

Thus, at that moment each tribe in unknown America was at war with each other tribe. At this moment there is not one hostile weapon used by one American against another, from Cape Bathurst at the north to the southern point of Patagonia.

At that moment Asia, Africa, and Europe were scenes of similar discord. Only, Europe herself knows so little of herself that no man would pretend to say which Longbeards were cutting the throats of other Longbeards, or which Scots were lying in ambush for which Britons, in any year of the first century of our era.

Call it the " Philosophy of History,"

or call it the " Providence of God," it is certain that the Humanity of the race of man has asserted itself as the Saviour of mankind said it should.

In this growing unity of mankind it has come about that the Sultan of Turkey cannot permit the massacre of Armenian Christians without answering for such permission before the world.

It has come about that no viceroy, serving a woman, who is the guardian of a boy, can be permitted to starve at his pleasure two hundred thousand of God's children. The world is so closely united — that is to say, unity is so real — that when such a viceroy does undertake to commit such an iniquity, somebody shall hold his hands. It has come to pass just now that this somebody is the United States of America.

Mr. Cleveland, when President of the United States, gave fair warning; he said that this sort of thing must stop, and that before long. The people who advised the mother, herself innocent, of the boy, who was also innocent, supposed that Mr. Cleveland did not mean what he said, and that the Nation called the United States did not mean what her servant said for her. They were mistaken. And the moment has come when the civilization of the world and its international law is to be advanced one step as they learn their mistake.

The mills of God grind slowly, yet they grind
exceeding small.

In this particular case it is the business of the United States to give to the millstone its last turn.

E. E. H.

# PREFACE TO THE EDITION OF 1897

THE publisher of this edition of "The Man without a Country" asks me to give some account of the circumstances and incidents of its publication. I do this with a certain reluctance, lest it should seem that I think they are more important than they are. It is true, however, that a series of curious coincidences accompanied the history of the story. Persons who are interested in the Curiosities of Literature, then, may read this preface, — and other persons are under no compulsion to do so.

The Civil War has taught its lesson so well that the average American of the year 1896 hardly understands that any such lesson was ever needed. The United States *is* a nation, now. And there is not left any one, living in the Northern, Middle, Western, or Pacific States, who ever thinks that the United States *are* a confederacy. The War settled that. But in 1862 men were obliged to make

speeches,—to write pamphlets and books,—
to show what now seems of course. And
any lesson was well received by persons of
conscience and patriotism, which showed
either positively or negatively what the
word "Patriotism" means,—or what one's
Country is.

Among other persons who did not seem to
know was an Ohio politician named Vallandigham. Perhaps he is living still. The
general reader of to-day would not know his
name, but that in some address he said that
he did not want to live in a country which
did something or other which the National
Administration, under Lincoln, had done.
General Ambrose Everett Burnside was then
in command of the Military Department in
which Mr. Vallandigham lived. With a
certain delicate wit and readiness which were
characteristic of the man, Burnside marked
his sense of the treasonable speech by sending Mr. Vallandigham with his compliments
to the Rebel general on the other side of
the Ohio, and saying that we wanted no
such people, and that the Rebel States were
welcome to him.

The letter and the present which went with
it of course engaged public attention in the
region where the transfer was made. The
Copperhead faction in Ohio, boldly and with

good political shrewdness, as it seems to me, accepted the issue, and named Mr. Vallandigham, — who was a martyr on their theory, — as their candidate for governor in the next election. He was exactly the fit candidate on the issue then before the people.

I was, at this time, furnishing political articles for the *Atlantic Monthly*. I had already conceived the idea of the " Man without a Country." I pressed the necessary work on it so that it might be published in the October number of the *Atlantic*, as my contribution to the Ohio canvass, as the election was to take place in October. But with a certain languor which attends the publication of most monthly journals, — a languor which seems to me an infelicity, — the publication was delayed until December, 1863, when Mr. Vallandigham had been beaten six weeks before by a majority of more than one hundred thousand, — and forgotten, till now, as long.

I say the idea had been conceived many months before, not to say many years before.

Napoleon the Great always had an idea that he had surrendered himself at Rochefort to Captain Maitland of the ship " Bellerophon," which ship received him after his overthrow. He sometimes undertook to maintain the absurd proposition that he was Maitland's personal captive, as in the Middle Ages one knight might have yielded himself as personal captive to another. This theory appears more than once in his invectives against the cruelty of the English Government in holding him at St. Helena.

The proposition seems to me absurd. It seemed so to the English Government, to the Prince Regent whom Napoleon addressed as "the most powerful, the most constant, and the most generous of my enemies." This was, by the way, the best thing the first gentleman in England ever had said of him — if only by good fortune it had been true. But whether absurd or not, it seems to me that it would have been good policy for the English Cabinet to have taken the fallen Emperor at his word. "Oh! you thought you were a guest on the 'Bellerophon'? We did not understand it so, but a guest on the 'Bellerophon' you shall be.

"Joiners, — upholsterers, — plumbers, — painters, — all of you, — fly round, — quick there, — make ready a fine cabin, — with sleeping rooms adjacent, — for our distinguished guest General Buonaparte. From this time he is the guest of the British people. He has come 'like Themistocles to seat himself by its hearth.' He has elected the 'Bellerophon' as the place. So let it be." Then from cruise to cruise, — of the "Bellerophon," — our distinguished guest would have been heard from thus : —

### NAVAL INTELLIGENCE

Sept. 30. H. M. Ship Bellerophon touched at the Cape, for water and mails. Our distinguished guest was in good health.

And then, six months after

June 11. Macao. H. M. Ship Bellerophon arrived for repairs, having lost a topmast in the typhoon. Our distinguished guest, Gen. Buonaparte, seemed to be well.

And, six months later

Botany Bay, Dec. 11. The corvette, Capt. Bell, reports that she spoke at sea H. M. S. Bellerophon. The Bellerophon made signal that all were well.

And so on, and so on. The "British people" could have stood it as long as the Emperor could.

What the British Government did was to consecrate St. Helena as a shrine for the worship of France for the next six years. It won for itself a general odium, such as it does not dislike, among all the nations of Europe. But if the Cabinet had happened to hear my plan, and had executed it, many apologies for its cruelty would have been unnecessary. They could say, "We did just

xix

what the Emperor expected, and what he asked for."

I may say in passing, that the English Cabinet has had more than one opportunity to take my advice, freely offered, and has, I think, always declined it.

Thus I had in my mind from the time when I read Scott's "Napoleon," a book not forgotten in my youth, the plan on which the story of poor dear Phil Nolan is constructed, —the story which is, at this present moment, in this reader's hands. The patriotic boys were singing a popular song, which said

"We'll hang Jeff Davis to a sour apple tree."

Jeff Davis, as it may not be remembered, was the leader of the Southern party. But I would say gently, "No, dear boys, we will not hang him to any tree. We will put him in comfortable quarters on the ' New Hampshire' ship of the line, and we will send him on her serial three-year voyages. Where she goes he shall go, and where she stays he shall stay."

Now the "New Hampshire" is a fine old square-sided, three or four decker, which is now a home for schoolboys, as may be seen by tourists in New York harbor. In those days she was thirty-three years newer or younger than she is now.

xx

With such motives, with such resources, and such principles, I began to read for the story of " The Man without a Country." I spent that summer in my old home at Worcester, — a " Western town in the heart of New England." I used, almost every morning, to report to my old friend, Mr. Samuel Foster Haven, the Librarian of the Antiquarian Society, one of the wisest, of the best-informed, and of the best men who ever lived. With me! his fine son — a surgeon in the 15th Massachusetts — had been killed the year before, while marching with the regiment in the battle of Fredericksburg. I would pass the time of day with Mr. Haven, and then go into Salisbury Hall, and read up for " The Man without a Country." As yet he had no name.

I read first the Reports of the Navy Department from 1798, when it was still a branch of the War Department, down to 1801. This was to be sure of my local color, and that I might never, by any accident, place a vessel in the place where she really was, or name an officer so that a real man could be annoyed. Shaw's name, Shubrick's name in the story, are naval names, — this was requisite for the color of the narrative. But there were no officers whom they fit. The " Levant " was a ship in our service.

But she had disappeared — no man knows where — oh! years before I introduced her on the top of the Andes. I will here say, — so careful are critics, — that among many readers of this story, only one, of whom I ever heard, observed that the "Levant," when Nolan died on her, was far inland. She had been placed on the top of the Andes intentionally.

I took such pains as this to be provided for defence, if any one should say, as the *New York Observer* did courteously, that I was a liar and a counterfeiter. Liars and counterfeiters do not intentionally place ships on the tops of mountains, and none but very ignorant editors think they do.

I took full notes of the names of officers and ships, to be ready for the detail of my story.

I then read, in full, all that I could find of Aaron Burr's two voyages down the Mississippi. It is not creditable to this country that there is no adequate history of Burr's attempt, whatever it was. I have sometimes thought that Mr. Jefferson himself did not wish to have any detail known. I am quite sure, after a good deal of study of the subject, that the officers of his Administration did not know every detail, nor one-half the details, nor one-fiftieth part of them.

The mines from which some competent historian will one day draw his most curious information as to Burr and his accomplices, are in the archives of the City of Mexico and of the cities of the Northern provinces of what was then the Viceroyalty of Mexico. Other information must be searched for in the city of Madrid. By a somewhat amusing accident, nearly forty years ago, the Spanish Government, in sending to the State of Louisiana some documents relating to its early history, unintentionally revealed the fact that General James Wilkinson, who commanded our forces for many years in the valley of the Mississippi, and who made Burr think that he was his accomplice, was in fact for many years in the pay of the Spanish governor at New Orleans. That Government understood the knack of governing better than Mr. Jefferson and his friends, who thought at that time that the world was governed too much. While Burr was organizing his expedition, the Spanish Government had its agents in every seaport city of the North. Their reports were faithfully transmitted to the governors of the Northern provinces, and some of them will be found in Santa Fé, in Austin, in San Antonio, in Monterey, and probably in Chihuahua, at this day.

Of all this, however, I knew nothing in the summer of 1863, nor did I need to know anything. I did read through the three volumes of General Wilkinson's " Memoirs," a very stupid galimatias of facts and of lies. I also read through the proceedings of Burr's trial at Richmond; there are not many people in the world who can say that. In the Antiquarian Library it was easy to find the side-lights, particularly in the newspaper files. Thus the Antiquarian Library is the only place where I could examine the newspapers of the period, describing Burr's journeys. These files were useful for bits of local color, — the name of a country-dance for instance.

The plan of the story is simple, and when once ready to write I wrote it, with my own hand, as I wrote then, almost without break. At the place where the author changes, and the story comes from Danforth's pen instead of Ingham's, I sent the copy to Mr. Fields of the *Atlantic* to ask him if it would do, and to explain why it must be printed immediately, if at all, and why printed without my name, in absolute secrecy. Fields sent back word at once that it would do, and that if he could have the rest of the copy at once it could go into the next number. I did finish it at once, I think in one sitting. The sen-

xxiv

timental reader may be interested to know
that my own tears blotted the paper of the
original manuscript.

Why it did not go into the October number
nor the November number, I think I never
knew. It was printed in the December
number, about the middle of November.
The first I knew of this was that I met
James Freeman Clarke at an evening party,
and he said to me, "Edward, we have
been reading your story and we like it very
much."

I said, "What story?"

He said, "The story of the Man without a
Country."

I said, "How did you know I wrote it?"

Clarke said, "Because it says so in the index
at the end of the number."

Between me and Fields the utmost caution
had been observed that the article should be
ascribed to Lieutenant Ingham, who is named
as its author in the text. But the manuscript
was in my handwriting, and the index-maker
at Cambridge had not been consulted as to
secrecy. He knew no reason why the world
should not know what he knew, so in making the annual index, which goes with the
December number, he innocently announced
my name. Mr. Fields' wish, and mine,
therefore, that the article might in some

quarters be ascribed to a naval officer was balked from the beginning by a well-meant blunder in the printing office.

The story took the public eye and interest. It met the taste of the patriotic public at the moment. It was copied everywhere without the slightest deference to copyright. It was, by the way, printed much more extensively in England than it was in America. Immediately there began to appear a series of speculations based on what you would have said was an unimportant error of mine. My hero is a purely imaginary character. The critics are right in saying that not only there never was such a man, but there never could have been such a man. But he had to have a name. And the choice of a name in a novel is a matter of essential importance, as it proved to be here.

I had a hero who was a young man in 1807. He knew nothing at that time but the valley of the Mississippi River. "He had been educated on a plantation where the finest company was a Spanish officer, or a French merchant from Orleans." He must have a name familiar to Western people at that time. Well, I remembered that in these preposterous memoirs of Wilkinson's, whenever he had a worse scrape than usual to explain, he would say that the papers were lost when Mr. Nolan was imprisoned or was killed in Texas. This Mr. Nolan, as Wilkinson generally calls him, had been engaged with Wilkinson in some speculations mostly relating to horses and almost always disreputable. Remembering this, I took the name Nolan for my hero. I made my man the real man's brother. "He had spent half his youth with an older brother, hunting horses in Texas." And again:—"he was catching wild horses in Texas with his adventurous cousin." I had the impression that Wilkinson's partner was named Stephen, and as Philip and Stephen were both evangelists in the Bible, as indeed I once heard a distinguished Episcopal divine preach a sermon about Philip on St. Stephen's day by accident, I named my man Philip Nolan, on the supposition that the mother who named one son Stephen would name another Philip. It was not for a year after, that, in looking at Wilkinson's "Memoirs" again, I found to my amazement, not to say my dismay, that Wilkinson's partner was named Philip Nolan. We had, therefore, two Philip Nolans, one a living historical character, who was shot by the Spaniards on the 21st of March, 1801, at Waco in Texas; the other a purely imaginary character invented by myself, who appears for the first time on the 23d of September, 1807, at a court-martial at Fort Adams.

Nobody but myself in New England had ever heard of Philip Nolan. But in the Southwest, in Texas and Louisiana, it was but sixty-two years since the Spaniards murdered him. In truth, it was the death of Nolan, the real Philip Nolan, killed by one Spanish governor while he held the safe-conduct of another, which roused that wave of indignation in the Southwest which ended in the independence of Texas. I think the State of Texas would do well, to-day, if it placed the statue of the real Phil Nolan in the Capitol at Washington by the side of that of Sam Houston.

Although we were at war, the *Atlantic* at once found its way into regions where the real Phil Nolan was known. A writer in the *New Orleans Picayune*, in a careful historical paper, explained at length that I had been mistaken all the way through, that Philip Nolan never went to sea, but to Texas. I received a letter from a lady in Baltimore who told me that two widowed sisters of his lived in that neighborhood. Unfortunately for me, this letter, written in perfectly good faith, was signed E. F. M. Fachtz. I was receiving many letters on the subject daily. I supposed that my correspondent was concealing her name, and was really "Eager for More Facts." When in reality I had the pleasure of meeting her a year or two afterwards, the two widowed sisters of the real Phil Nolan were both dead.

But in 1876 I was fortunate enough, on the kind invitation of Mr. Miner, to visit his family in their beautiful plantation at Terre Bonne. There I saw an old negro who was a boy when Master Phil Nolan left the old plantation on the Mississippi River for the last time. Master Phil Nolan had then married Miss Fanny Lintot, who was, I think, the aunt of my host. He permitted me to copy the miniature of the young adventurer.

I have since done my best to repair the error by which I gave Philip Nolan's name to another person, by telling the story of his fate in a book called "Philip Nolan's Friends." For the purpose of that book, I studied the history of Miranda's attempt against Spain, and of John Adams's preparations for a descent of the Mississippi River. The professional historians of the United States are very reticent in their treatment of these themes. At the time when John Adams had a little army at Cincinnati, ready to go down and take New Orleans, there were no Western correspondents to the Eastern Press.

Within a year after the publication of the
"Man without a Country" in the *Atlantic*,
more than half a million copies of the story
had been printed in America and in England.
I had curious accounts from the army and
navy, of the interest with which it was read
by gentlemen on duty. One of our officers
lent the *Atlantic* to a lady in the Miner
family. She ran into the parlor, crying out,
"Here is a man who knows all about uncle
Phil Nolan." An Ohio officer, who entered
the city of Jackson, in Mississippi, with Grant,
told me that he went at once to the State
House. Matters were in a good deal of
confusion there, and he picked up from the
floor a paper containing the examination of
*Philip Nolan*, at Walnut Springs, the old
name of Vicksburg. This was before the
real Philip's last expedition. The United
States authorities, in the execution of the
neutrality laws, had called him to account,
and had made him show the evidence that
he had the permission of the Governor of
New Orleans for his expedition.

In 1876 I visited Louisiana and Texas, to
obtain material for "Philip Nolan's Friends,"
which was published that year as a serial in
*Scribner's Magazine*. I obtained there several
autographs of the real Phil Nolan, — and the
original Spanish record of one of the trials of

the survivors of his party, — a trial which resulted in the cruel execution of Ephraim Blackburn, seven years after he was arrested. That whole transaction, wholly ignored by all historians of the United States known to me, is a sad blot on the American administration of the Spanish kings. Their excuse is the confusion of everything in Madrid between 1801 and 1807. The hatred of the Mexican authorities among our frontiersmen of the Southwest is largely due to the dishonor and cruelty of those transactions.

The Navy Department was occasionally asked what records it had of Phil Nolan's exile. Naturally, the gentlemen there did not like to confess ignorance. I was told, perhaps truly, that the answer generally given there was that "there was an officer kept on foreign service all his life, but that his name was not Nolan." A fine old friend of mine, an officer of marines, said seriously, when he read the story, that it was queer that while he had served on half the vessels in the service, he had never met this man. Another dear old friend of mine, president of a historical society, remembered the court-martial at Fort Adams very well. I am afraid no one else had any record of it. Admiral Davis was good enough to tell me that the term "felucca" is not used outside the Straits of Gibraltar, — and in the recent editions, as in this, the " felucca " with slaves is a " schooner." With one or two other such corrections the story in the reader's hands is the same as that published in the *Atlantic*, in 1863.

About twenty years ago, it was translated into German, with the omission of one or two passages, and published in a German journal. As soon as this magazine arrived here the story was retranslated, and reprinted as a German addition to American history, by the editor of the *American Magazine*. This was after half-a-million copies had been printed, in the English language. The accident is an excellent illustration of the truth, that thus far no book has ever been published. It is to be wished that " publishers " could be made to understand this.

I learned, to my great pleasure, that it was translated into Spanish, and printed in Peru for the encouragement of the patriots of that country in their contest with Chile.

I have been glad to learn that it has proved a useful reading-book in the higher classes of the schools in Minnesota, in Wisconsin, and other States.

EDWARD E. HALE.

# THE MAN WITHOUT A COUNTRY.

 SUPPOSE that very few casual readers of the " New York Herald " of August 13, 1863, observed, in an obscure corner, among the " Deaths," the announcement, —

" NOLAN. Died, on board U. S. Corvette " Levant," Lat. 2° 11′ S., Long. 131° W., on the 11th of May, PHILIP NOLAN."

I happened to observe it, because I was stranded at the old Mission House in Mackinaw, waiting for a Lake Superior steamer which did not choose to come, and I was devouring to the very stubble all the current literature I could get hold of, even down to the deaths and marriages in the " Herald." My memory for names and people is good, and the reader will see, as he goes on, that I had reason enough to remember Philip Nolan. There are hundreds of readers who would have paused at that announcement, if the officer of the

"Levant" who reported it had chosen to make it thus: "Died, May 11, THE MAN WITHOUT A COUNTRY." For it was as "The Man without a Country" that poor Philip Nolan had generally been known by the officers who had him in charge during some fifty years, as, indeed, by all the men who sailed under them. I dare say there is many a man who has taken wine with him once a fortnight, in a three years' cruise, who never knew that his name was "Nolan," or whether the poor wretch had any name at all.

There can now be no possible harm in telling this poor creature's story. Reason enough there has been till now, ever since Madison's administration went out in 1817, for very strict secrecy, the secrecy of honor itself, among the gentlemen of the navy who have had Nolan in successive charge. And certainly it speaks well for the *esprit de corps* of the profession, and the personal honor of its members, that to the press this man's story has been wholly unknown, — and, I think, to the coun-

2

try at large also. I have reason to
think, from some investigations I made
in the Naval Archives when I was at-
tached to the Bureau of Construction,
that every official report relating to him
was burned when Ross burned the
public buildings at Washington. One
of the Tuckers, or possibly one of the
Watsons, had Nolan in charge at the
end of the war; and when, on returning
from his cruise, he reported at Washington to one of the Crowninshields,
— who was in the Navy Department
when he came home, — he found that
the Department ignored the whole
business. Whether they really knew
nothing about it, or whether it was a
"*Non mi ricordo*," determined on as a
piece of policy, I do not know. But
this I do know, that since 1817, and
possibly before, no naval officer has
mentioned Nolan in his report of a
cruise.

But, as I say, there is no need for
secrecy any longer. And now the poor
creature is dead, it seems to me worth
while to tell a little of his story, by way

3

of showing young Americans of to-day what it is to be A MAN WITHOUT A COUNTRY.

PHILIP NOLAN was as fine a young officer as there was in the "Legion of the West," as the Western division of our army was then called. When Aaron Burr made his first dashing expedition down to New Orleans in 1805, at Fort Massac, or somewhere above on the river, he met, as the Devil would have it, this gay, dashing, bright young fellow; at some dinner-party, I think. Burr marked him, talked to him, walked with him, took him a day or two's voyage in his flat-boat, and, in short, fascinated him. For the next year, barrack-life was very tame to poor Nolan. He occasionally availed himself of the permission the great man had given him to write to him. Long, high-worded, stilted letters the poor boy wrote and rewrote and copied. But never a line did he have in reply from the gay deceiver. The other boys in the garrison sneered at him, because he

4

sacrificed in this unrequited affection for a politician the time which they devoted to Monongahela, hazard, and high-low-jack. Bourbon, euchre, and poker were still unknown. But one day Nolan had his revenge. This time Burr came down the river, not as an attorney seeking a place for his office, but as a disguised conqueror. He had defeated I know not how many district-attorneys; he had dined at I know not how many public dinners; he had been heralded in I know not how many Weekly Arguses, and it was rumored that he had an army behind him and an empire before him. It was a great day — his arrival — to poor Nolan. Burr had not been at the fort an hour before he sent for him. That evening he asked Nolan to take him out in his skiff, to show him a canebrake or a cotton-wood tree, as he said, — really to seduce him; and by the time the sail was over, Nolan was enlisted body and soul. From that time, though he did not yet know it, he lived as A MAN WITHOUT A COUNTRY.

5

What Burr meant to do I know no more than you, dear reader. It is none of our business just now. Only, when the grand catastrophe came, and Jefferson and the House of Virginia of that day undertook to break on the wheel all the possible Clarences of the then House of York, by the great treason trial at Richmond, some of the lesser fry in that distant Mississippi Valley, which was farther from us than Puget's Sound is to-day, introduced the like novelty on their provincial stage; and, to while away the monotony of the summer at Fort Adams, got up, for *spectacles*, a string of court-martials on the officers there. One and another of the colonels and majors were tried, and, to fill out the list, little Nolan, against whom, Heaven knows, there was evidence enough, — that he was sick of the service, had been willing to be false to it, and would have obeyed any order to march any-whither with any one who would follow him had the order been signed, " By command of His Exc. A. Burr." The courts dragged on. The big
6

flies escaped, — rightly for all I know.
Nolan was proved guilty enough, as I
say ; yet you and I would never have
heard of him, reader, but that, when the
president of the court asked him at the
close whether he wished to say anything
to show that he had always been faith-
ful to the United States, he cried out,
in a fit of frenzy, —

" Damn the United States ! I wish I
may never hear of the United States
again ! "

I suppose he did not know how the
words shocked old Colonel Morgan,
who was holding the court. Half the
officers who sat in it had served through
the Revolution, and their lives, not to
say their necks, had been risked for the
very idea which he so cavalierly cursed
in his madness. He, on his part, had
grown up in the West of those days,
in the midst of " Spanish plot," " Orleans plot," and all the rest. He had
been educated on a plantation where
the finest company was a Spanish officer or a French merchant from Orleans.
His education, such as it was, had been

perfected in commercial expeditions to
Vera Cruz, and I think he told me his
father once hired an Englishman to be a
private tutor for a winter on the plantation. He had spent half his youth
with an older brother, hunting horses
in Texas; and, in a word, to him "United States" was scarcely a reality. Yet
he had been fed by "United States"
for all the years since he had been in
the army. He had sworn on his faith
as a Christian to be true to "United
States." It was "United States" which
gave him the uniform he wore, and
the sword by his side. Nay, my poor
Nolan, it was only because "United
States" had picked you out first as
one of her own confidential men of
honor that "A. Burr" cared for you
a straw more than for the flat-boat men
who sailed his ark for him. I do not
excuse Nolan; I only explain to the
reader why he damned his country, and
wished he might never hear her name
again.

He never did hear her name but once
again. From that moment, Sept. 23,

8

1807, till the day he died, May 11, 1863, he never heard her name again. For that half-century and more he was a man without a country.

Old Morgan, as I said, was terribly shocked. If Nolan had compared George Washington to Benedict Arnold, or had cried, "God save King George," Morgan would not have felt worse. He called the court into his private room, and returned in fifteen minutes, with a face like a sheet, to say, —

"Prisoner, hear the sentence of the Court! The Court decides, subject to the approval of the President, that you never hear the name of the United States again."

Nolan laughed. But nobody else laughed. Old Morgan was too solemn, and the whole room was hushed dead as night for a minute. Even Nolan lost his swagger in a moment. Then Morgan added, —

"Mr. Marshal, take the prisoner to Orleans in an armed boat, and deliver him to the naval commander there."

9

The marshal gave his orders and the prisoner was taken out of court.

"Mr. Marshal," continued old Morgan, "see that no one mentions the United States to the prisoner. Mr. Marshal, make my respects to Lieutenant Mitchell at Orleans, and request him to order that no one shall mention the United States to the prisoner while he is on board ship. You will receive your written orders from the officer on duty here this evening. The court is adjourned without day."

I have always supposed that Colonel Morgan himself took the proceedings of the court to Washington city, and explained them to Mr. Jefferson. Certain it is that the President approved them, — certain, that is, if I may believe the men who say they have seen his signature. Before the "Nautilus" got round from New Orleans to the Northern Atlantic coast with the prisoner on board, the sentence had been approved, and he was a man without a country.

The plan then adopted was substantially the same which was necessarily followed

10

ever after. Perhaps it was suggested
by the necessity of sending him by
water from Fort Adams and Orleans.
The Secretary of the Navy — it must
have been the first Crowninshield,
though he is a man I do not remember — was requested to put Nolan on
board a government vessel bound on
a long cruise, and to direct that he
should be only so far confined there
as to make it certain that he never saw
or heard of the country. We had few
long cruises then, and the navy was
very much out of favor; and as almost
all of this story is traditional, as I have
explained, I do not know certainly what
his first cruise was. But the commander to whom he was intrusted, —
perhaps it was Tingey or Shaw, though
I think it was one of the younger
men, — we are all old enough now, —
regulated the etiquette and the pre-
cautions of the affair, and according to
his scheme they were carried out, I
suppose, till Nolan died.

When I was second officer of the " Intrepid," some thirty years after, I saw

the original paper of instructions. I
have been sorry ever since that I did
not copy the whole of it. It ran, however, much in this way: —

"WASHINGTON (with a date, which
must have been late in 1807).

"SIR, — You will receive from Lieutenant
Neale the person of Philip Nolan, late a
lieutenant in the United States Army.

"This person on his trial by court-martial
expressed, with an oath, the wish that he
might 'never hear of the United States
again.'

"The Court sentenced him to have his wish
fulfilled.

"For the present, the execution of the
order is intrusted by the President to this
Department.

"You will take the prisoner on board your
ship, and keep him there with such precau-
tions as shall prevent his escape.

"You will provide him with such quarters,
rations, and clothing as would be proper for
an officer of his late rank, if he were a pas-
senger on your vessel on the business of his
Government.

"The gentlemen on board will make any
arrangements agreeable to themselves regarding his society. He is to be exposed to no
12

indignity of any kind, nor is he ever unnecessarily to be reminded that he is a prisoner.

"But under no circumstances is he ever to hear of his country or to see any information regarding it ; and you will especially caution all the officers under your command to take care, that, in the various indulgences which may be granted, this rule, in which his punishment is involved, shall not be broken.

"It is the intention of the Government that he shall never again see the country which he has disowned. Before the end of your cruise you will receive orders which will give effect to this intention.

"Respectfully yours,

"W. SOUTHARD, for the

"Secretary of the Navy."

If I had only preserved the whole of this paper, there would be no break in the beginning of my sketch of this story. For Captain Shaw, if it were he, handed it to his successor in the charge, and he to his, and I suppose the commander of the "Levant" has it to-day as his authority for keeping this man in this mild custody. The rule adopted on board the ships on which I have met "the man with-

out a country" was, I think, transmitted from the beginning. No mess
liked to have him permanently, because his presence cut off all talk of
home or of the prospect of return, of
politics or letters, of peace or of war,
— cut off more than half the talk men
liked to have at sea. But it was always thought too hard that he should
never meet the rest of us, except to
touch hats, and we finally sank into
one system. He was not permitted
to talk with the men, unless an officer
was by. With officers he had unre-
strained intercourse, as far as they and
he chose. But he grew shy, though
he had favorites: I was one. Then
the captain always asked him to dinner
on Monday. Every mess in succes-
sion took up the invitation in its turn.
According to the size of the ship, you
had him at your mess more or less
often at dinner. His breakfast he ate
in his own state-room, — he always
had a state-room, — which was where
a sentinel or somebody on the watch
could see the door. And whatever
14

else he ate or drank, he ate or drank
alone. Sometimes, when the marines
or sailors had any special jollification,
they were permitted to invite "Plain-
Buttons," as they called him. Then
Nolan was sent with some officer, and
the men were forbidden to speak of
home while he was there. I believe
the theory was that the sight of his
punishment did them good. They
called him "Plain-Buttons," because,
while he always chose to wear a regu-
lation army-uniform, he was not permitted to wear the army-button, for
the reason that it bore either the initials
or the insignia of the country he had
disowned.

I remember, soon after I joined the
navy, I was on shore with some of
the older officers from our ship and
from the "Brandywine," which we had
met at Alexandria. We had leave to
make a party and go up to Cairo and
the Pyramids. As we jogged along
(you went on donkeys then), some of
the gentlemen (we boys called them
"Dons," but the phrase was long since

changed) fell to talking about Nolan, and some one told the system which was adopted from the first about his books and other reading. As he was almost never permitted to go on shore, even though the vessel lay in port for months, his time at the best hung heavy; and everybody was permitted to lend him books, if they were not published in America and made no allusion to it. These were common enough in the old days, when people in the other hemisphere talked of the United States as little as we do of Paraguay. He had almost all the foreign papers that came into the ship, sooner or later; only somebody must go over them first, and cut out any advertisement or stray paragraph that alluded to America. This was a little cruel sometimes, when the back of what was cut out might be as innocent as Hesiod. Right in the midst of one of Napoleon's battles, or one of Canning's speeches, poor Nolan would find a great hole, because on the back of the page of that paper there had

16

been an advertisement of a packet for New York, or a scrap from the President's message. I say this was the first time I ever heard of this plan, which afterwards I had enough and more than enough to do with. I remember it, because poor Phillips, who was of the party, as soon as the allusion to reading was made, told a story of something which happened at the Cape of Good Hope on Nolan's first voyage; and it is the only thing I ever knew of that voyage. They had touched at the Cape, and had done the civil thing with the English Admiral and the fleet, and then, leaving for a long cruise up the Indian Ocean, Phillips had borrowed a lot of English books from an officer, which, in those days, as indeed in these, was quite a windfall. Among them, as the Devil would order, was the " Lay of the Last Minstrel," which they had all of them heard of, but which most of them had never seen. I think it could not have been published long. Well, nobody thought there could be any risk of

17

anything national in that, though Phillips swore old Shaw had cut out the "Tempest" from Shakespeare before he let Nolan have it, because he said "the Bermudas ought to be ours, and, by Jove, should be one day." So Nolan was permitted to join the circle one afternoon when a lot of them sat on deck smoking and reading aloud. People do not do such things so often now; but when I was young we got rid of a great deal of time so. Well, so it happened that in his turn Nolan took the book and read to the others; and he read very well, as I know. Nobody in the circle knew a line of the poem, only it was all magic and Border chivalry, and was ten thousand years ago. Poor Nolan read steadily through the fifth canto, stopped a minute and drank something, and then began, without a thought of what was coming, —

> "Breathes there the man, with soul so dead,
> Who never to himself hath said," —

It seems impossible to us that anybody ever heard this for the first time;

18

but all these fellows did then, and poor
Nolan himself went on, still unconsciously or mechanically, —

"This is my own, my native land!"

Then they all saw something was to
pay; but he expected to get through,
I suppose, turned a little pale, but
plunged on, —

"Whose heart hath ne'er within him burned,
As home his footsteps he hath turned
From wandering on a foreign strand?—
If such there breathe, go, mark him well,"—

By this time the men were all beside
themselves, wishing there was any way
to make him turn over two pages; but
he had not quite presence of mind for
that; he gagged a little, colored crim-
son, and staggered on, —

"For him no minstrel raptures swell;
High though his titles, proud his name,
Boundless his wealth as wish can claim,
Despite these titles, power, and pelf,
The wretch, concentred all in self,"—

and here the poor fellow choked, could
not go on, but started up, swung the
book into the sea, vanished into his

state-room, "And by Jove," said Phillips, "we did not see him for two months again. And I had to make up some beggarly story to that English surgeon why I did not return his Walter Scott to him."

That story shows about the time when Nolan's braggadocio must have broken down. At first, they said, he took a very high tone, considered his imprisonment a mere farce, affected to enjoy the voyage, and all that; but Phillips said that after he came out of his state-room he never was the same man again. He never read aloud again, unless it was the Bible or Shakespeare, or something else he was sure of. But it was not that merely. He never entered in with the other young men exactly as a companion again. He was always shy afterwards, when I knew him, — very seldom spoke, unless he was spoken to, except to a very few friends. He lighted up occasionally, — I remember late in his life hearing him fairly eloquent on something which had been suggested to him by

20

one of Fléchier's sermons, — but generally he had the nervous, tired look
of a heart-wounded man.

When Captain Shaw was coming home,
— if, as I say, it was Shaw, — rather
to the surprise of everybody they made
one of the Windward Islands, and lay
off and on for nearly a week. The
boys said the officers were sick of salt-
junk, and meant to have turtle-soup
before they came home. But after
several days the "Warren" came to
the same rendezvous; they exchanged
signals; she sent to Phillips and
these homeward-bound men letters and
papers, and told them she was out-
ward-bound, perhaps to the Mediterranean, and took poor Nolan and his
traps on the boat back to try his
second cruise. He looked very blank
when he was told to get ready to join
her. He had known enough of the
signs of the sky to know that till that
moment he was going "home." But
this was a distinct evidence of something he had not thought of, perhaps, — that there was no going home

21

for him, even to a prison. And this was the first of some twenty such transfers, which brought him sooner or later into half our best vessels, but which kept him all his life at least some hundred miles from the country he had hoped he might never hear of again.

It may have been on that second cruise, — it was once when he was up the Mediterranean, — that Mrs. Graff, the celebrated Southern beauty of those days, danced with him. They had been lying a long time in the Bay of Naples, and the officers were very intimate in the English fleet, and there had been great festivities, and our men thought they must give a great ball on board the ship. How they ever did it on board the " Warren " I am sure I do not know. Perhaps it was not the " Warren," or perhaps ladies did not take up so much room as they do now. They wanted to use Nolan's state-room for something, and they hated to do it without asking him to the ball; so the captain said they might ask him, if they would be responsible that he did not talk with the wrong people, "who would give him intelligence." So the dance went on, the finest party that had ever been known, I dare say; for I never heard of a man-of-war ball that was not. For ladies they had the family of the American consul, one or two travellers who had adventured so far, and a nice bevy of English girls and matrons, perhaps Lady Hamilton herself.

Well, different officers relieved each other in standing and talking with Nolan in a friendly way, so as to be sure that nobody else spoke to him. The dancing went on with spirit, and after a while even the fellows who took this honorary guard of Nolan ceased to fear any *contretemps*. Only when some English lady — Lady Hamilton, as I said, perhaps — called for a set of "American dances," an odd thing happened. Everybody then danced contra-dances. The black band, nothing loath, conferred as to what "American dances" were, and started off with

23

"Virginia Reel," which they followed with "Money-Musk," which, in its turn in those days, should have been followed by "The Old Thirteen." But just as Dick, the leader, tapped for his fiddles to begin, and bent forward, about to say, in true negro state, "'The Old Thirteen,' gentlemen and ladies!" as he had said "'Virginny Reel,' if you please!" and "'Money-Musk,' if you please!" the captain's boy tapped him on the shoulder, whispered to him, and he did not announce the name of the dance; he merely bowed, began on the air, and they all fell to, — the officers teaching the English girls the figure, but not telling them why it had no name.

But that is not the story I started to tell. As the dancing went on, Nolan and our fellows all got at ease, as I said, — so much so, that it seemed quite natural for him to bow to that splendid Mrs. Graff, and say, —

"I hope you have not forgotten me, Miss Rutledge. Shall I have the honor of dancing?"

He did it so quickly, that Fellows, who was with him, could not hinder him. She laughed and said, —

" I am not Miss Rutledge any longer, Mr. Nolan ; but I will dance all the same," just nodded to Fellows, as if to say he must leave Mr. Nolan to her, and led him off to the place where the dance was forming.

Nolan thought he had got his chance. He had known her at Philadelphia, and at other places had met her, and this was a Godsend. You could not talk in contra-dances, as you do in cotillions, or even in the pauses of waltzing ; but there were chances for tongues and sounds, as well as for eyes and blushes. He began with her travels, and Europe, and Vesuvius, and the French ; and then, when they had worked down, and had that long talking time at the bottom of the set, he said boldly, — a little pale, she said, as she told me the story years after, —

" And what do you hear from home, Mrs. Graff ? "

And that splendid creature looked through him. Jove! how she must have looked through him!

"Home!! Mr. Nolan!!! I thought you were the man who never wanted to hear of home again!"—and she walked directly up the deck to her husband, and left poor Nolan alone, as he always was. — He did not dance again. I cannot give any history of him in order; nobody can now; and, indeed, I am not trying to.

These are the traditions, which I sort out, as I believe them, from the myths which have been told about this man for forty years. The lies that have been told about him are legion. The fellows used to say he was the "Iron Mask;" and poor George Pons went to his grave in the belief that this was the author of "Junius," who was being punished for his celebrated libel on Thomas Jefferson. Pons was not very strong in the historical line.

A happier story than either of these I have told is of the war. That came

along soon after. I have heard this
affair told in three or four ways, — and,
indeed, it may have happened more
than once. But which ship it was on I
cannot tell. However, in one, at least,
of the great frigate-duels with the English, in which the navy was really bap-
tized, it happened that a round-shot
from the enemy entered one of our
ports square, and took right down the
officer of the gun himself, and almost
every man of the gun's crew. Now
you may say what you choose about
courage, but that is not a nice thing to
see. But, as the men who were not
killed picked themselves up, and as
they and the surgeon's people were
carrying off the bodies, there appeared
Nolan, in his shirt-sleeves, with the
rammer in his hand, and, just as if he
had been the officer, told them off with
authority, — who should go to the cock-
pit with the wounded men, who should
stay with him, — perfectly cheery, and
with that way which makes men feel
sure all is right and is going to be right.
And he finished loading the gun with

27

his own hands, aimed it, and bade the men fire. And there he stayed, captain of that gun, keeping those fellows in spirits, till the enemy struck, — sitting on the carriage while the gun was cooling, though he was exposed all the time, — showing them easier ways to handle heavy shot, — making the raw hands laugh at their own blunders, — and when the gun cooled again, getting it loaded and fired twice as often as any other gun on the ship. The captain walked forward by way of encouraging the men, and Nolan touched his hat and said, —

"I am showing them how we do this in the artillery, sir."

And this is the part of the story where all the legends agree; the commodore said, —

"I see you do, and I thank you, sir; and I shall never forget this day, sir, and you never shall, sir."

And after the whole thing was over, and he had the Englishman's sword, in the midst of the state and ceremony of the quarter-deck, he said, —

28

"Where is Mr. Nolan? Ask Mr. Nolan to come here."

And when Nolan came, he said, —

"Mr. Nolan, we are all very grateful to you to-day; you are one of us to-day; you will be named in the despatches."

And then the old man took off his own sword of ceremony, and gave it to Nolan, and made him put it on. The man told me this who saw it. Nolan cried like a baby, and well he might. He had not worn a sword since that infernal day at Fort Adams. But always afterwards on occasions of ceremony, he wore that quaint old French sword of the commodore's.

The captain did mention him in the despatches. It was always said he asked that he might be pardoned. He wrote a special letter to the Secretary of War. But nothing ever came of it. As I said, that was about the time when they began to ignore the whole transaction at Washington, and when Nolan's imprisonment began to carry itself on because there was nobody to

29

stop it without any new orders from
home.

I have heard it said that he was with
Porter when he took possession of the
Nukahiwa Islands. Not this Porter,
you know, but old Porter, his father,
Essex Porter, — that is, the old Essex
Porter, not this Essex. As an artillery officer, who had seen service in
the West, Nolan knew more about
fortifications, embrasures, ravelins,
stockades, and all that, than any of
them did; and he worked with a right
good-will in fixing that battery all
right. I have always thought it was
a pity Porter did not leave him in
command there with Gamble. That
would have settled all the question
about his punishment. We should
have kept the islands, and at this
moment we should have one station
in the Pacific Ocean. Our French
friends, too, when they wanted this
little watering-place, would have found
it was preoccupied. But Madison and
the Virginians, of course, flung all that
away.

30

All that was near fifty years ago. If Nolan was thirty then, he must have been near eighty when he died. He looked sixty when he was forty. But he never seemed to me to change a hair afterwards. As I imagine his life, from what I have seen and heard of it, he must have been in every sea, and yet almost never on land. He must have known, in a formal way, more officers in our service than any man living knows. He told me once, with a grave smile, that no man in the world lived so methodical a life as he. "You know the boys say I am the Iron Mask, and you know how busy he was." He said it did not do for any one to try to read all the time, more than to do anything else all the time; but that he read just five hours a day. "Then," he said, "I keep up my note-books, writing in them at such and such hours from what I have been reading; and I include in these my scrap-books." These were very curious indeed. He had six or eight, of different subjects. There was one of

31

History, one of Natural Science, one which he called "Odds and Ends." But they were not merely books of extracts from newspapers. They had bits of plants and ribbons, shells tied on, and carved scraps of bone and wood, which he had taught the men to cut for him, and they were beautifully illustrated. He drew admirably. He had some of the funniest drawings there, and some of the most pathetic, that I have ever seen in my life. I wonder who will have Nolan's scrap-books.

Well, he said his reading and his notes were his profession, and that they took five hours and two hours respectively of each day. "Then," said he, "every man should have a diversion as well as a profession. My Natural History is my diversion." That took two hours a day more. The men used to bring him birds and fish, but on a long cruise he had to satisfy himself with centipedes and cockroaches and such small game. He was the only naturalist I ever met who knew anything about the habits of the house-fly and the

32

mosquito. All those people can tell
you whether they are *Lepidoptera* or
*Steptopotera*; but as for telling how
you can get rid of them, or how they
get away from you when you strike
them, — why Linnæus knew as little
of that as John Foy the idiot did.
These nine hours made Nolan's regular daily "occupation." The rest of
the time he talked or walked. Till he
grew very old, he went aloft a great
deal. He always kept up his exercise;
and I never heard that he was ill. If
any other man was ill, he was the
kindest nurse in the world; and he
knew more than half the surgeons do.
Then if anybody was sick or died, or
if the captain wanted him to, on any
other occasion, he was always ready to
read prayers. I have said that he read
beautifully.

My own acquaintance with Philip
Nolan began six or eight years after
the English war, on my first voyage
after I was appointed a midshipman.
It was in the first days after our Slave-
Trade treaty, while the Reigning

33

House, which was still the House of Virginia, had still a sort of sentimentalism about the suppression of the horrors of the Middle Passage, and something was sometimes done that way. We were in the South Atlantic on that business. From the time I joined, I believe I thought Nolan was a sort of lay chaplain, — a chaplain with a blue coat. I never asked about him. Everything in the ship was strange to me. I knew it was green to ask questions, and I suppose I thought there was a "Plain-Buttons" on every ship. We had him to dine in our mess once a week, and the caution was given that on that day nothing was to be said about home. But if they had told us not to say anything about the planet Mars or the Book of Deuteronomy, I should not have asked why; there were a great many things which seemed to me to have as little reason. I first came to understand anything about "the man without a country" one day when we overhauled a dirty little schooner which

34

had slaves on board. An officer was sent to take charge of her, and, after a few minutes, he sent back his boat to ask that some one might be sent him who could speak Portuguese. We were all looking over the rail when the message came, and we all wished we could interpret, when the captain asked Who spoke Portuguese. But none of the officers did; and just as the captain was sending forward to ask if any of the people could, Nolan stepped out and said he should be glad to interpret, if the captain wished, as he understood the language. The captain thanked him, fitted out another boat with him, and in this boat it was my luck to go. When we got there, it was such a scene as you seldom see, and never want to. Nastiness beyond account, and chaos run loose in the midst of the nastiness. There were not a great many of the negroes; but by way of making what there were understand that they were free, Vaughan had had their hand-cuffs and ankle-cuffs knocked off, and, for convenience' sake, was

35

putting them upon the rascals of the schooner's crew. The negroes were, most of them, out of the hold, and swarming all round the dirty deck, with a central throng surrounding Vaughan and addressing him in every dialect, and *patois* of a dialect, from the Zulu click up to the Parisian of Beledeljereed.

As we came on deck, Vaughan looked down from a hogshead, on which he had mounted in desperation, and said : —

" For God's love, is there anybody who can make these wretches understand something ? The men gave them rum, and that did not quiet them. I knocked that big fellow down twice, and that did not soothe him. And then I talked Choctaw to all of them together ; and I 'll be hanged if they understood that as well as they understood the English."

Nolan said he could speak Portuguese, and one or two fine-looking Kroomen were dragged out, who, as it had been found already, had worked for the

36

Portuguese on the coast at Fernando Po.

"Tell them they are free," said Vaughan; "and tell them that these rascals are to be hanged as soon as we can get rope enough."

Nolan "put that into Spanish,"—that is, he explained it in such Portuguese as the Kroomen could understand, and they in turn to such of the negroes as could understand them. Then there was such a yell of delight, clinching of fists, leaping and dancing, kissing of Nolan's feet, and a general rush made to the hogshead by way of spontaneous worship of Vaughan, as the *deus ex machina* of the occasion.

"Tell them," said Vaughan, well pleased, "that I will take them all to Cape Palmas."

This did not answer so well. Cape Palmas was practically as far from the homes of most of them as New Orleans or Rio Janeiro was; that is, they would be eternally separated from home there. And their interpreters, as we could understand, instantly said, "*Ah, non*

37

*Palmas,*" and began to propose infinite
other expedients in most voluble language. Vaughan was rather disap-
pointed at this result of his liberality,
and asked Nolan eagerly what they
said. The drops stood on poor
Nolan's white forehead, as he hushed
the men down, and said : —

"He says, 'Not Palmas.' He says,
'Take us home, take us to our own
country, take us to our own house,
take us to our own pickaninnies and our
own women.' He says he has an old
father and mother who will die if they
do not see him. And this one says he
left his people all sick, and paddled
down to Fernando to beg the white
doctor to come and help them, and
that these devils caught him in the bay
just in sight of home, and that he has
never seen anybody from home since
then. And this one says," choked out
Nolan, "that he has not heard a word
from his home in six months, while he
has been locked up in an infernal bar-
racoon."

Vaughan always said he grew gray himself while Nolan struggled through this interpretation. I, who did not understand anything of the passion involved in it, saw that the very elements were melting with fervent heat, and that something was to pay somewhere. Even the negroes themselves stopped howling, as they saw Nolan's agony, and Vaughan's almost equal agony of sympathy. As quick as he could get words, he said : —

" Tell them yes, yes, yes ; tell them they shall go to the Mountains of the Moon, if they will. If I sail the schooner through the Great White Desert, they shall go home ! "

And after some fashion Nolan said so. And then they all fell to kissing him again, and wanted to rub his nose with theirs.

But he could not stand it long ; and getting Vaughan to say he might go back, he beckoned me down into our boat. As we lay back in the stern-sheets and the men gave way, he said to me : " Youngster, let that show you what it is to be without a family, with-

39

out a home, and without a country.
And if you are ever tempted to say a
word or to do a thing that shall put a
bar between you and your family, your
home, and your country, pray God in
his mercy to take you that instant
home to his own heaven. Stick by
your family, boy; forget you have a
self, while you do everything for them.
Think of your home, boy; write and
send, and talk about it. Let it be
nearer and nearer to your thought, the
farther you have to travel from it; and
rush back to it when you are free, as
that poor black slave is doing now.
And for your country, boy," and the
words rattled in his throat, "and for
that flag," and he pointed to the ship,
"never dream a dream but of serving
her as she bids you, though the service
carry you through a thousand hells.
No matter what happens to you, no
matter who flatters you or who abuses
you, never look at another flag, never
let a night pass but you pray God to
bless that flag. Remember, boy, that
behind all these men you have to do

40

with, behind officers, and government, and people even, there is the Country Herself, your Country, and that you belong to Her as you belong to your own mother. Stand by Her, boy, as you would stand by your mother, if those devils there had got hold of her to-day!"

I was frightened to death by his calm, hard passion; but I blundered out that I would, by all that was holy, and that I had never thought of doing anything else. He hardly seemed to hear me; but he did, almost in a whisper, say: "O, if anybody had said so to me when I was of your age!"

I think it was this half-confidence of his, which I never abused, for I never told this story till now, which afterward made us great friends. He was very kind to me. Often he sat up, or even got up, at night, to walk the deck with me, when it was my watch. He explained to me a great deal of my mathematics, and I owe to him my taste for mathematics. He lent me books, and helped me about my reading. He never alluded so directly to his story again; but from one and another officer I have learned, in thirty years, what I am telling. When we parted from him in St. Thomas harbor, at the end of our cruise, I was more sorry than I can tell. I was very glad to meet him again in 1830; and later in life, when I thought I had some influence in Washington, I moved heaven and earth to have him discharged. But it was like getting a ghost out of prison. They pretended there was no such man, and never was such a man. They will say so at the Department now! Perhaps they do not know. It will not be the first thing in the service of which the Department appears to know nothing!

There is a story that Nolan met Burr once on one of our vessels, when a party of Americans came on board in the Mediterranean. But this I believe to be a lie; or, rather, it is a myth, *ben trovato*, involving a tremendous blowing-up with which he sunk Burr, — asking him how he liked to be "without a country." But it is clear from Burr's life, that nothing of the sort could have happened; and I mention this only as an illustration of the stories which get a-going where there is the least mystery at bottom.

So poor Philip Nolan had his wish fulfilled. I know but one fate more dreadful; it is the fate reserved for those men who shall have one day to exile themselves from their country because they have attempted her ruin, and shall have at the same time to see the prosperity and honor to which she rises when she has rid herself of them and their iniquities. The wish of poor Nolan, as we all learned to call him, not because his punishment was too great, but because his repentance was so clear, was precisely the wish of every Bragg and Beauregard who broke a soldier's oath two years ago, and of every Maury and Barron who broke a sailor's. I do not know how often they have repented. I do know that they have done all that in them lay that they might have no country,— that all the honors, as-

43

sociations, memories, and hopes which belong to " country" might be broken up into little shreds and distributed to the winds. I know, too, that their punishment, as they vegetate through what is left of life to them in wretched Boulognes and Leicester Squares, where they are destined to upbraid each other till they die, will have all the agony of Nolan's, with the added pang that every one who sees them will see them to despise and to execrate them. They will have their wish, like him.

For him, poor fellow, he repented of his folly, and then, like a man, submitted to the fate he had asked for. He never intentionally added to the difficulty or delicacy of the charge of those who had him in hold. Accidents would happen; but they never happened from his fault. Lieutenant Truxton told me that, when Texas was annexed, there was a careful discussion among the officers, whether they should get hold of Nolan's handsome set of maps and cut Texas out of it, — from the map of the world and the map of

Mexico. The United States had been cut out when the atlas was bought for him. But it was voted, rightly enough, that to do this would be virtually to reveal to him what had happened, or, as Harry Cole said, to make him think Old Burr had succeeded. So it was from no fault of Nolan's that a great botch happened at my own table, when, for a short time, I was in command of the George Washington corvette, on the South American station. We were lying in the La Plata, and some of the officers, who had been on shore and had just joined again, were entertaining us with accounts of their misadventures in riding the half-wild horses of Buenos Ayres. Nolan was at table, and was in an unusually bright and talkative mood. Some story of a tumble reminded him of an adventure of his own when he was catching wild horses in Texas with his adventurous cousin, at a time when he must have been quite a boy. He told the story with a good deal of spirit, — so much so, that the silence which often follows a good story hung over the table for an instant, to be broken by Nolan himself. For he asked perfectly unconsciously : —

" Pray, what has become of Texas ? After the Mexicans got their independence, I thought that province of Texas would come forward very fast. It is really one of the finest regions on earth ; it is the Italy of this continent. But I have not seen or heard a word of Texas for near twenty years."

There were two Texan officers at the table. The reason he had never heard of Texas was that Texas and her affairs had been painfully cut out of his newspapers since Austin began his settlements ; so that, while he read of Honduras and Tamaulipas, and, till quite lately, of California, — this virgin province, in which his brother had travelled so far, and, I believe, had died, had ceased to be to him. Waters and Williams, the two Texas men, looked grimly at each other and tried not to laugh. Edward Morris had his attention attracted by the third link in the chain of the captain's chandelier. Watrous was seized with a convulsion of sneezing. Nolan himself saw that something was to pay, he did not know what. And I, as master of the feast had to say,—

"Texas is out of the map, Mr. Nolan. Have you seen Captain Back's curious account of Sir Thomas Roe's Welcome?"

After that cruise I never saw Nolan again. I wrote to him at least twice a year, for in that voyage we became even confidentially intimate; but he never wrote to me. The other men tell me that in those fifteen years he *aged* very fast, as well he might indeed, but that he was still the same gentle, uncomplaining, silent sufferer that he ever was, bearing as best he could his self-appointed punishment,— rather less social, perhaps, with new men whom he did not know, but more anxious, apparently, than ever to serve and befriend and teach the boys, some of whom fairly seemed to worship him. And now it seems the dear old fellow is dead. He has found a home at last, and a country.

47

Since writing this, and while consider-ing whether or no I would print it, as a warning to the young Nolans and Vallandighams and Tatnalls of to-day of what it is to throw away a country, I have received from Danforth, who is on board the "Levant," a letter which gives an account of Nolan's last hours. It removes all my doubts about telling this story.

To understand the first words of the let-ter, the non-professional reader should remember that after 1817, the position of every officer who had Nolan in charge was one of the greatest delicacy. The government had failed to renew the order of 1807 regarding him. What was a man to do? Should he let him go? What, then, if he were called to account by the Department for violating the order of 1807? Should he keep him? What, then, if Nolan should be liberated some day, and should bring an action for false im-prisonment or kidnapping against every man who had had him in charge? I urged and pressed this upon Southard, and I have reason to think that other officers did the same thing. But the Secretary always said, as they so often do at Washington, that there were no special orders to give, and that we must act on our own judgment. That means, "If you succeed, you will be sustained; if you fail, you will be disavowed." Well, as Danforth says, all that is over now, though I do not know but I expose myself to a criminal prosecution on the evidence of the very revelation I am making.

Here is the letter: —

"Levant, 2° 2' S. @ 131° W.

"Dear Fred: — I try to find heart and life to tell you that it is all over with dear old Nolan. I have been with him on this voyage more than I ever was, and I can understand wholly now the way in which you used to speak of the dear old fellow. I could see that he was not strong, but I had no idea the end was so near. The doctor has been watching him very carefully, and yesterday morning came to

me and told me that Nolan was not
so well, and had not left his state-
room, — a thing I never remember
before. He had let the doctor come
and see him as he lay there, — the first
time the doctor had been in the state-
room, — and he said he should like to
see me. Oh, dear! do you remember
the mysteries we boys used to invent
about his room in the old 'Intrepid'
days? Well, I went in, and there, to
be sure, the poor fellow lay in his
berth, smiling pleasantly as he gave
me his hand, but looking very frail.
I could not help a glance round, which
showed me what a little shrine he had
made of the box he was lying in. The
stars and stripes were triced up above
and around a picture of Washington,
and he had painted a majestic eagle,
with lightnings blazing from his beak
and his foot just clasping the whole
globe, which his wings overshadowed.
The dear old boy saw my glance, and
said, with a sad smile, ' Here, you see,
I have a country!' And then he
pointed to the foot of his bed, where
50

I had not seen before a great map of the United States, as he had drawn it from memory, and which he had there to look upon as he lay. Quaint, queer old names were on it, in large letters: 'Indiana Territory,' 'Mississippi Territory,' and 'Louisiana Territory,' as I suppose our fathers learned such things: but the old fellow had patched in Texas, too; he had carried his western boundary all the way to the Pacific, but on that shore he had defined nothing.

"'O Danforth,' he said, 'I know I am dying. I cannot get home. Surely you will tell me something now? — Stop! stop! Do not speak till I say what I am sure you know, that there is not in this ship, that there is not in America, — God bless her! — a more loyal man than I. There cannot be a man who loves the old flag as I do, or prays for it as I do, or hopes for it as I do. There are thirty-four stars in it now, Danforth. I thank God for that, though I do not know what their names are. There has never been one taken away: I thank God for that. I

51

know by that that there has never been any successful Burr. O Danforth, Danforth,' he sighed out, 'how like a wretched night's dream a boy's idea of personal fame or of separate sovereignty seems, when one looks back on it after such a life as mine! But tell me, — tell me something, — tell me everything, Danforth, before I die!'

"Ingham, I swear to you that I felt like a monster that I had not told him everything before. Danger or no danger, delicacy or no delicacy, who was I, that I should have been acting the tyrant all this time over this dear, sainted old man, who had years ago expiated, in his whole manhood's life, the madness of a boy's treason? 'Mr. Nolan,' said I, 'I will tell you everything you ask about. Only, where shall I begin?'

"Oh, the blessed smile that crept over his white face! and he pressed my hand and said, 'God bless you!' 'Tell me their names,' he said, and he pointed to the stars on the flag. 'The last I know is Ohio. My father lived in

Kentucky. But I have guessed Mich-igan and Indiana and Mississippi, — that was where Fort Adams is, — they make twenty. But where are your other fourteen ? You have not cut up any of the old ones, I hope ? '

" Well, that was not a bad text, and I told him the names in as good order as I could, and he bade me take down his beautiful map and draw them in as I best could with my pencil. He was wild with delight about Texas, told me how his cousin died there ; he had marked a gold cross near where he supposed his grave was ; and he had guessed at Texas. Then he was de-lighted as he saw California and Ore-gon ; — that, he said, he had suspected partly, because he had never been per-mitted to land on that shore, though the ships were there so much. 'And the men,' said he, laughing, 'brought off a good deal besides furs.' Then he went back — heavens, how far ! — to ask about the Chesapeake, and what was done to Barron for surrendering her to the Leopard, and whether Burr ever tried again, — and he ground his teeth with the only passion he showed. But in a moment that was over, and he said, 'God forgive me, for I am sure I forgive him.' Then he asked about the old war, — told me the true story of his serving the gun the day we took the Java, — asked about dear old David Porter, as he called him. Then he settled down more quietly, and very happily, to hear me tell in an hour the history of fifty years.

"How I wished it had been somebody who knew something! But I did as well as I could. I told him of the English war. I told him about Fulton and the steamboat beginning. I told him about old Scott, and Jackson; told him all I could think of about the Mississippi, and New Orleans, and Texas, and his own old Kentucky. And do you think, he asked who was in command of the 'Legion of the West.' I told him it was a very gallant officer named Grant, and that, by our last news, he was about to establish his head-quarters at Vicksburg.

Then, 'Where was Vicksburg?' I
worked that out on the map; it was
about a hundred miles, more or less,
above his old Fort Adams; and I
thought Fort Adams must be a ruin
now. 'It must be at old Vick's plantation, at Walnut Hills,' said he: 'well,
that is a change!'

"I tell you, Ingham, it was a hard
thing to condense the history of half
a century into that talk with a sick
man. And I do not now know what
I told him, — of emigration, and the
means of it, — of steamboats, and rail-
roads, and telegraphs, — of inventions,
and books, and literature, — of the
colleges, and West Point, and the
Naval School, — but with the queerest
interruptions that ever you heard. You
see it was Robinson Crusoe asking all
the accumulated questions of fifty-six
years!

"I remember he asked, all of a sudden,
who was President now; and when I
told him, he asked if Old Abe was
General Benjamin Lincoln's son. He
said he met old General Lincoln, when

55

he was quite a boy himself, at some Indian treaty. I said no, that Old Abe was a Kentuckian like himself, but I could not tell him of what family; he had worked up from the ranks. 'Good for him!' cried Nolan; 'I am glad of that. As I have brooded and wondered, I have thought our danger was in keeping up those regular successions in the first families.' Then I got talking about my visit to Washington. I told him of meeting the Oregon Congressman, Harding; I told him about the Smithsonian, and the Exploring Expedition; I told him about the Capitol, and the statues for the pediment, and Crawford's Liberty, and Greenough's Washington: Ingham, I told him everything I could think of that would show the grandeur of his country and its prosperity; but I could not make up my mouth to tell him a word about this infernal rebellion!

" And he drank it in and enjoyed it as I cannot tell you. He grew more and more silent, yet I never thought he was tired or faint. I gave him a glass of water, but he just wet his lips, and told me not to go away. Then he asked me to bring the Presbyterian 'Book of Public Prayer,' which lay there, and said, with a smile, that it would open at the right place, — and so it did. There was his double red mark down the page; and I knelt down and read, and he repeated with me, 'For ourselves and our country, O gracious God, we thank Thee, that, notwithstanding our manifold transgressions of Thy holy laws, Thou hast continued to us Thy marvellous kindness,' — and so to the end of that thanksgiving. Then he turned to the end of the same book, and I read the words more familiar to me: 'Most heartily we beseech Thee with Thy favor to behold and bless Thy servant, the President of the United States, and all others in authority,' — and the rest of the Episcopal collect. 'Danforth,' said he, 'I have repeated those prayers night and morning, it is now fifty-five years.' And then he said he would go to sleep.

57

He bent me down over him and kissed me; and he said, ' Look in my Bible, Danforth, when I am gone.' And I went away.

" But I had no thought it was the end. I thought he was tired and would sleep. I knew he was happy, and I wanted him to be alone.

" But in an hour, when the doctor went in gently, he found Nolan had breathed his life away with a smile. He had something pressed close to his lips. It was his father's badge of the Order of the Cincinnati.

" We looked in his Bible, and there was a slip of paper at the place where he had marked the text : —

" ' They desire a country, even a heavenly : wherefore God is not ashamed to be called their God : for He hath prepared for them a city.'

" On this slip of paper he had written :

" ' Bury me in the sea; it has been my home, and I love it. But will not some one set up a stone for my mem-

ory at Fort Adams or at Orleans, that
my disgrace may not be more than I
ought to bear?   Say on it: —

" ' In Memory of

" 'PHILIP NOLAN,

" ' Lieutenant in the Army of the United States.

" ' He loved his country as no other man has
loved her ; but no man deserved less at
her hands.' "

59

Date Due

JY 7 48